The
Freaky Joe
Club

Other books by P. J. McMahon

The Freaky Joe Club

Secret File #1:
The Mystery of the Swimming Gorilla

Secret File #2:
The Case of the Smiling Shark

Secret File #3:
The Mystery of the Morphing Hockey Stick

Illustrated by
John Manders

The Freaky Joe Club

Secret File #4:
The Case of the Psychic Hamster

by
P. J. McMahon

ALADDIN PAPERBACKS
New York   London   Toronto   Sydney

To Joshua Giraffe—One Great Guy
— P. J. M.

❧ALADDIN PAPERBACKS
An imprint of Simon & Schuster Children's Publishing Division
1230 Avenue of the Americas, New York, NY 10020
Text copyright © 2005 by Patricia McMahon
Illustrations copyright © 2005 by John Manders
All rights reserved, including the right of
reproduction in whole or in part in any form.
ALADDIN PAPERBACKS and colophon are registered
trademarks of Simon & Schuster, Inc.
Designed by Lisa Vega
The text of this book was set in 14-point Minion.
Manufactured in the United States of America
First Aladdin Paperbacks edition February 2005
10 9 8 7 6 5 4 3 2 1
Library of Congress Control Number 2004114445
ISBN 0-689-86263-6

Table of Contents

Chapter One

A Terrible Decision Must Be Made

I have to write it all down. This is my job. As leader of this Freaky Joe Club, I record our adventures. So once again I open the lock, unwind the bicycle chain that circles the book, and carefully, carefully, open the cover.

The old pages at the beginning must be turned slowly. I go to the end. And admire the pictures of a hockey stick, hockey gloves, and a red ball. I drew these to illustrate important points of our third adventure. Considering the fact that my mom is the artist in our family, I didn't do too badly. Okay, few kids have fingers that long. But other than that, the pictures are okay. And our tales must be written down so one day the word can be passed on.

Now I will write of our latest adventure. The fourth case of this Freaky Joe Club. Can I possibly fit it all in a few pages? There's so much to tell. So many questions. And so much homework. I should follow Freaky Joe's Rule Number Three B: Begin at the Beginning. But when did it start? Even before school began? When I made that fateful prediction? On the day we first saw the sign? On that summer's afternoon in The Secret Place when I had to make a terrible decision?

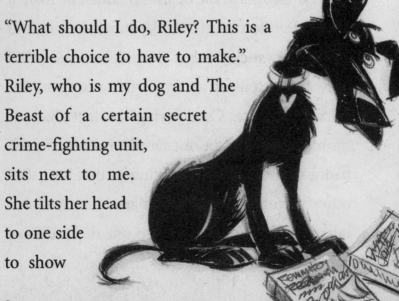

"What should I do, Riley? This is a terrible choice to have to make." Riley, who is my dog and The Beast of a certain secret crime-fighting unit, sits next to me. She tilts her head to one side to show me she is thinking big doggy thoughts about my problem.

Two important books lie side by side on the floor of The Secret Place, headquarters of the Freaky Joe Club. Not the Book, the actual real and true secret files. No, these are the two other important books.

"Come on, girl, help me. I only have one more day after this before school starts. One day when I have nothing to do but read a good mystery. But I don't know what to do. See, this is the newest book in the Remington Reedmarsh, Lemur Detective series." I show Riley the cover, with Remington bravely fighting the Terrible Tyrant Tyler, a marsupial of enormous size.

"I've been waiting and waiting for this. And Mom found it today at the Big Blue Bookstore. But I've already read chapter one of *The Secret of the Mysterious Disappearing Joust.*" I let Riley have a sniff of the latest adventure of Sir

Chester the Clever, Knight Detective. She licks the picture of Chuck, Sir Chester's squire.

"I like Chuck too," I tell her. "And I've never ever *ever* not finished a book once I started. But I've been waiting for the new Remington Reedmarsh!"

Riley rolls on her back, puts all four legs in the air, and moans. This must be a dog's way of saying "This is a hard decision." Reaching a paw out, she swats the picture of Sir Chester and Chuck.

Which reminds me of Freaky Joe's Rule Number Twenty-Four B: A Freaky Joe Club Member Is Always Loyal.

"Good idea, girl. Stick with Sir Chester and Chuck. I'll read Remington Reedmarsh this weekend. I mean, nothing much can happen the first week of school, right?"

I pick up Sir Chester again and turn to the page where he was speaking to the fair Lady Mary Rose.

• • • •

"Sir Chester, Sir Chester, doth thou not hearest a word I say?" Lady Mary Rose asks as she hits Sir Chester on his helmet.

"Conor, Conor, you are not listening to me." The Queen of China smacketh my head in the same fashion.

"I was listening to you," I promise. What was she saying?

"Well, then, can we go?" My little sister does handstands while asking her question. She is, of course, not really the Queen of China. But sometimes she can act like she wants to be the first five-year-old in charge of the world.

"Go where?"

"To school! To see the lists! On the doors! The lists you told me about! The list with my name on it and my teacher's name on it! Because I'm a big girl who is going to kindergarten very, very soon!"

I'm pretty sure that's what she's saying. It's a little hard to be sure because Bella is turning cartwheels as she talks.

"But you have to go, too, that's what Mommy says! And you said we could go! To school!"

Oh.

"Bella," I explain, "the lists go on the door at exactly four o'clock. We have to wait till then."

"What time is it now?" Bella holds up one finger, two fingers, three fingers, her head tilted to the side like Riley.

"It is almost time." Which should give me enough time to read at least two more chapters.

"Tell me one of your stories about Chuck," Bella insists. "I like Chuck."

"I can't tell you about Chuck yet. This is a new book," I explain.

"Tell me an old one."

"I don't want to, I want to read this new Chuck." I wave the book in the air to make my point.

"Then tell me about the animal I'm going to turn into."

Huh?

"Huh?" I ask.

"You said it!" Bella jumps up. "You said it!" she says. Again.

With my special big brother senses, I detect that Bella is moving into the Frustrated Zone. Alarms should be going off. Danger. "You said when I go to school I will turn into an animal like you."

"Huh?"

A member of the Freaky Joe Club is always clear.

"*Conor!* You are not being fair." Bella jumps up and down. Sirens begin to wail. Big Danger.

"I'm not being not fair. I'm being mixed up. 'Cause I never said you would turn into an animal at school. It's not a magic school, it's the Edith R. Hammerrocker Elementary School."

"Yes! And I will turn into an animal. You said," Bella repeats.

Here it is. At last. My biggest mystery ever. The Case of the Completely Confusing Little Chinese Sister.

"I said?"

"I don't think I want to change. And Mugsy says she isn't going to school, so who cares." Mugsy is Bella's best friend and, possibly, an evil genius.

"Are you sure Mugsy didn't say you would become an animal?" The detective is desperate for a clue.

"*No!*"

A helpful answer.

"You did. You said 'Almost time for kindergarten. Soon you will turn into an animal.'"

The detective is completely confused. Where is Chuck when you need him?

"Bella, I . . ." The sound of my words is lost.

Bang!

The door to The Secret Place flies open.

Clang!

It hits the metal pie plate that is behind the door. A useful metal pie plate. Useful for preventing large holes in the wall.

Two creatures burst into the room at the same time.

Riley leaps to her feet, barking.

The creatures hold their hands, palms out, in front of them. Twenty fingers are wiggling.

"Hmmmmm. Hmmmmm. Hmmmmm!" they shout. If a noise like that can be described as shouting.

Annoying might be more correct.

"I was actually in the door first," one of them says.

"No way, José," says the other.

"My name is not José, and you know it," says the first.

"What are you being?" Bella asks.

"We're Hamsters. We're Hamsters," they cry.

"That's it!" Bella announces. "I'm going to turn into a hamster."

Huh?

Chapter Two
It's a Sign! It's a Sign!

"How is Bella going to turn into a real hamster?" one of the creatures asks. The creature named Jack.

"Is that possible? Can she do it? Did you read how to do that in one of your books?" Jack stalks around the room, fingers snapping, brain working. Well, sort of. Working in the way Jack's brain works.

It is important to remember that this is the secret agent who suggested that the members of the Freaky Joe Club should carry a spare eyeball at all times.

"Wait a minute." Jack pauses, turns, and points his finger at me. "Will she be a Bella-size hamster, or an itty-bitty little hamster?"

"If she's an itty-bitty hamster," says the other hamster creature, secret agent Timmy, "she could be an important crime-fighting secret weapon."

"Oh yeah," Jack agrees. "We could stick her down sink pipes, and she could crawl along dark, dirty pipes dripping with icky stuff till she came to the little window where the bad guys are planning really big bad-guy stuff, and she could listen and . . ."

"No, Mugsy always wants to play that game. I'm tired of it," Bella tells us. "I want to turn into a unicorn. I'll be Stella Starbright."

"Just how are you going to turn her into an animal, Conor?" Jack swings around and points his whole arm at me. "Cough it up."

"Cough up what?" Timmy asks. "A fur ball?" He grabs *Animals of the World, Volume I* from our Secret Agents Library. "I wonder, do hamsters have fur balls?"

Right about now, I would rather be riding away

on a steed alongside Sir Chester and Chuck, looking for fierce dragons.

"Conor, you are not turning me into a hamster. If you do, I'll tell Mom, and she'll stop painting a big yellow wall and be very mad at you."

I think it is time to explain some basic facts to the members of the Freaky Joe Club. And my sister.

"Anyway, Jack and Timmy don't look like hamsters," Bella finishes.

"That would be because they aren't hamsters." I decide to begin with the obvious. "And you are not going to turn into one."

"But you said . . . ," Bella begins.

"But you said . . . ," Jack continues.

"Okay, time for a snack," Timmy says, pulling something sort of orange out of his pocket.

"Bella, all our schools have nicknames for their students," I explain. "Like a team name."

"Like we are Octopi when we swim," Bella says.

"Right. But you don't turn into an octopus when you swim."

"Oh, wouldn't that be good!" Jack flops to the floor. He appears to be trying to swim and fly, with his arms and legs. "Watch out, octopus coming through."

"But you're missing four more legs," Timmy points out. "Maybe you could carry them around with you, like your extra eyeball."

"Good idea," Jack answers as he squinches across the floor. Riley crawls along on her belly next to him.

Any octopus looking on would probably cry.

I try again.

"Bella, our school's nickname is the Hammer-rocker Hamsters. Jack and Timmy were giving the Hammerrocker Hamster Hello that we sometimes do at school ."

"So I say I'm a hamster, but I stay a girl." Bella figures it out.

"You mean you don't know how to turn your sister into a cute little hamster?" Jack asks in a disappointed voice.

"I don't know how to turn anyone into any animal," I inform them.

"That would be the most cool thing in the world, if you could." Jack paces again, fingers snapping.

"I want to go see the lists." Bella gets back to the original subject.

"I hope we're back in the same class," Jack says. "It wasn't cool in school when we weren't in the same class."

"I know." Timmy takes something from the orange food group out of his mouth. "Last year, I had to sit next to Mad Dog at lunch, and he always ate everything. It was no fun."

"And this year we can use the secret signs in school. That'll be good." Jack begins to flap his arm up and down. He resembles the giant secretary bird of Southern Africa attempting to fly.

I may not be able to turn anyone into an animal, but I do know my species.

"I asked my mom to ask Mrs. Burton if we could be in the same class," I report.

"What'd she say?" Timmy asks.

"Mrs. B. laughed. A lot."

"Who laughed?" Bella asks.

"Mrs. Burton, Mrs. Roslyn Burton," I answer.

"Our principal," Timmy adds. "She's really funny."

"You'll like her," I tell Bella. "She wears bright-colored dresses and cloth wrapped around her head."

"I'll like her," Bella promises.

"She's the Head Hamster," Jack tells her. "It's too bad you won't get to see her."

"What do you mean, Jack?" I ask.

"You know, the sign." Jack the octopus flops back down on the floor.

"Let me help, Jack," Timmy says. "Was it red, with the letters S-T-O-P?"

"No," Jack says. "The sign outside the school with the big news. Duh!"

Huh?

Chapter Three
What Is a Zoot Zumwalt?

"What exactly is the news, Jack?" I ask.

"Important stuff," he says.

I use my special crime-fighting secret agent ability to figure out that Jack doesn't remember exactly what the sign said.

"We will go and read it," I announce.

"To the bicycles!" Timmy shouts.

We run, we race, we ride.

On her Magical Baby Katie Unicorn bicycle, Bella manages to beat Jack.

"A new land-speed record!" Timmy shouts as we pull up at the front of the school.

"I let her win," Jack whispers to me. "To be nice."

"Thanks," I tell Jack. Even if I don't believe him.

"Conor, what does it say? I can't read it," Bella complains.

"Because it's hard to read upside down." I turn her right side up.

"No good," she says. "I don't know how to read."

I tell her what it says. "'Edith R. Hammerrocker Elementary School Welcomes Our New Principal Mr. Alvino "Zoot" Zumwalt.'"

"Zoot Zumwalt?" Timmy says.

"He sounds like he could be fast." Jack thinks. "That could be good."

"Depends on

19

whether he's trying to catch you," I say.

"Do you think he will wear pretty dresses and a scarf on his head?" Bella asks.

"That could be bad." Jack thinks some more. "Unless it was like one of those motorcycle rider scarves. Maybe he'll ride up to school on this enormous motorcycle." Jack holds imaginary handlebars high above his head and makes loud *zoom-zoom*ing noises.

"Doesn't sound like a school principal," Timmy says.

"That's what would make it so cool," Jack explains.

"Mugsy would like him then," Bella says.

"Let's find out what's going on," I suggest. "Maybe there's some information over by the lists."

"And we can find out who I sit next to at lunch." Timmy rubs his hands together.

. . . .

Kids, kids, and more kids crowd around the big glass doors at the front of the school. Parents, who are tall enough to see over them, lean in as well. Dropping our bicycles next to the flag post, we head over.

"I'll help you check out your class first," I tell Bella.

A loud moan sounds from up near the front.

"Lambert!"

"Someone's got Ms. Lambert," Jack says.

"I like Ms. Lambert," I protest.

"Could that be because Ms. Lambert likes you?" Jack answers. "Could we use the word *Teacher's Pet*?"

"That's two words," I tell him.

"Is a Teacher's Pet a hamster?" Bella wants to know.

"Bella, over here," Mugsy calls out, jumping up

and down so Bella can see her. As she is dressed in army camouflage with a helmet on, she is hard to miss.

"What does it say?" Bella asks, pointing at the list.

"I can't read," Mugsy says.

"That's why you go to school," Bella explains.

"I still don't want to go," Mugsy tells her.

"You don't turn into an animal," Bella informs Mugsy.

"But that was the only part I liked," Mugsy moans.

I scan down the kindergarten list to find *Bella Moloney* a few lines below *Mugsy Magoolaghan*.

"Well, you two are in the same class," I tell them. "You have Miss Carly Gray."

"Will we like Miss Carly Gray?" Bella asks.

"Oh, you girls are lucky," Mad Dog's mother answers as she turns from checking a list. "She is so sweet. She likes kids a lot."

"Yuck," says Mugsy.

It seems a good idea, at least to me, for a teacher to be someone who likes kids. I don't get it about mean teachers. I mean, why take the job? Did no one tell them the schools were full of kids? I imagine a teacher bursting into the principal's office on the first day:

"Excuse me, but I have a Big Problem. My class- room is full of little kids!"

"Oh, just go back and be mean to them," says the principal.

"Conor, you're here!" Jack's yelling gets my attention.

"Me, too?" Timmy asks.

Mad Dog scoots over to us. "I'm in Mr. Lefty's class!" he tells his mom.

"That is Mr. Lawal," his mother answers.

"You too, Conor. And Jack and Timmy and Murphy," Mad Dog goes on.

Well, all right. Mr. Harlan "Lefty" Lawal.

"I can't believe Mrs. Burton won't be here," Mad Dog's mom is telling another mom. "I mean, I'm happy for her that she's been promoted to that great new job."

I concentrate my special secret agent listening skills.

"But I do wonder about this Mr. Zumwalt, who used to be at Barker's Landing Elementary," Mad Dog's mother continues. She looks around, then leans in to whisper, "When he was introduced at the big district PTO meeting, he said he was sure everyone would understand that he had to come here because of the Hamsters."

"He was probably just being nice," the other mom says. "By *Hamsters* he means our darling children. Who wouldn't want to come work with our talented children?"

"Conor, you have to come see this," Jack calls me. "Matthew Eads can make himself burp five times in a row."

"I can do seven," Mugsy says.

Everyone rushes to see this feat. Bella walks over on her hands.

Mugsy's sister, Murphy, carries their little brother, Mikey, upside down. She's shaking him. "He says he ate a bug."

"It was a little green bug," Mikey says.

I watch Matthew burp five times in a row, which I must admit is impressive.

And I think Mrs. Burton would have thought so too.

I wonder what Mr. Zumwalt will be like. What was it Mad Dog's mom said? He's coming because of the Hamsters.

Huh?

Chapter Four

Oh, We Are Marching to the Hammerrocker

"Listen up! I need all children to pay attention to me now!" My mom, who definitely has green spots all over her, shouts through cupped hands as she hops onto the back bumper of the Ship's Cove Security truck—the truck that drives around our neighborhood making sure everything is A-OK in Ship's Cove.

Actually, it's the truck that drives around Ship's Cove making sure everything is A-OK with the dogs of Ship's Cove. For this truck is driven by Bubba Butowski, ace security guard and friend of dogs everywhere.

Bubba stands now by the side of the truck, which has banners hung on the sides. One banner reads THE HAMMERROCKER EXPRESS and the other claims HAMSTERS ROCK. Bubba is wearing his back-to-school outfit: a big yellow T-shirt reading SCHOOL RULES! On his head, he wears a pointy sort of wizard's hat, which is covered with letters of the alphabet.

"Just give me the word, Riley's mom," Bubba tells my mom.

"One second to go!" she shouts again. "This is your last friendly warning. Gather behind the banner now."

My mom climbs down, picking up a large pole as she does. The pole holds one end of a long banner. Mrs. Magoolaghan picks up the other end. In big, bright green letters it reads SHIP'S COVE STUDENTS SAILING BACK TO SCHOOL!!!

The green letters definitely match the green spots on my mother.

My mom is an artist who paints big paintings. And banners for the swim team, field day, our birthdays, and the back-to-school parade. All the kids march behind Bubba's truck and my mom's sign.

"If you have to go back to school, you may as well go back in style, sweeties," is how my mother explains the idea.

"Okay, Big Guys," Bubba calls. "Almost time to go. Who is so good at waiting? What smart dogs! Do you want a treat for being such good dogs? Who're the good dogs?"

The back of the truck is filled with our Riley; Mrs. Bailey's Napoleon; Smidgen; Butter the big Dalmatian; the Quinns' new dog, Casey; and the two greyhounds Rosie and Nellie. All of them are wearing the same pointy-shaped hats covered with letters. Smidgen has on a little yellow shirt to match Bubba's. "This is a hard day for them,"

Bubba explains. "To see the children go."

Bubba wipes the corner of his eye. He climbs in and turns on the engine. The light circles round. With new backpacks on and new lunch boxes in our hands, we line up behind the truck and the banner.

On the top of Bella's head sits a very large pink-and-purple bow. I

remember asking my mother to promise that she would not let Bella wear this bow outside the house.

Mugsy still wears camouflage.

"Hamsters, forward march!" my mother cries. "Molly, set the pace."

Molly McGuire is our school janitor. And a folk singer. She sings a line, and we shout it back.

"I don't know but I've been told,
Hamster kids are mighty bold.
Now they're back in school again,
armed with pencils and with pen.
Gonna learn 'bout many things,
maybe even learn to sing."

Riley and Butter join in, howling as loud as can be.

"Hamsters are the very best, can't waste time singing 'bout the rest!"

"HAMMERRROCKER HAMSTERS! HAM-MERROCKER HAMSTERS!" we shout.

The parade turns left onto Buccaneer's Boulevard and up to the front door of the school, where the marching, chanting, Ship's Cove Back-to-School Parade finally comes to a halt.

Students arriving on buses cheer. The kids in the march cheer. The dogs howl. The ace security guard driving the truck honks the horn.

And a man comes running over, in a funny, Bent at the Waist, Knees Up sort of run. He holds a clipboard in one hand and waves his arms up and down, up and down.

Jack gives me an elbow to the side. "Conor, he's giving a secret sign! Which one is it? Is he someone we should know?"

"That couldn't be you-know-who, could it?" Timmy asks.

"Jack, there is no secret sign that involves

flapping like a bird," I explain for the 1,167th time. "If you move your arms like airplane wings, it means *come quick*."

"He's coming quick," Timmy points out.

The running man flaps his way to the front of the parade, waving his clipboard around. "What is this? What is this?" he calls out as he stops right next to the truck, the dogs, Bubba, and my mother and her banner.

"Don't worry, I'm just delivering the Hamsters," my mom says, putting out a green-spotted hand for him to shake.

This makes the banner dip over to one side. Which does make it droop on the man's head a bit.

Which makes him panic a bit.

"Hamsters? Hamsters? Where?" he shouts as he tries to escape from the banner.

"Sorry about that," my mother apologizes as she unwraps the sheet from his head. "Hamsters here," she says, waving her arm over the parade.

"Are you talking about the kids who go to my school?" the man asks in a loud voice. Now that he is not running or jumping back, I realize he is one tall adult. He's lots taller than my mom, with long, skinny arms and legs that seem to twitch in all directions at the same time.

He reminds me of the rare giant praying mantis, the Bammerama bug, found in the northeast corner of upper Tasmania. I read about them in *Bugs of the World,* of course.

"Your school?" my mom asks.

"I am Mr. Alvino Zumwalt, the new principal of the school." He spreads his long arms wide. "I'm here to make things better. I am in charge."

"Nice to meet you, Mr. Zumwalt. I'm in charge of two kids in your school." My mom tries to shake Mr. Zumwalt's hand but it keeps flying out of reach. She jumps once or twice, then gives up.

"What are these dogs doing here?" Mr. Zumwalt asks. He still looks a bit confused, if you ask me. "These dogs should not be here. There are no dogs on the schedule," he says, checking his clipboard. His voice keeps going up and up, louder and louder.

"Don't worry, they're just part of the parade," my mom explains. She's using the You Should Stay Calm voice she uses on Bella sometimes.

"Who said you could have a parade?" Mr. Zumwalt begins to flap again.

"I said we could have a parade," my mother answers.

Uh-oh. Mom is tapping her foot.

"I don't want dogs at my school," Mr. Zumwalt says in a loud voice. Riley begins to bark. So does Butter. And Rosie. Smidgen, who is the size of a coffee cup, begins to growl, bares her teeth, and shakes her head, making her hat fly off.

Bubba hops out of the truck. The point on the

top of his hat is bent over to one side. "I think you might want to keep your voices down a little," he announces. "I think you might be scaring the poor, little dogs. Did that man scare you, did he, huh? Do y'all need a treat?" Bubba dives back into the truck to get more dog biscuits.

"Who was that?" Mr. Zumwalt asks.

"Bubba!" all the kids in the parade shout.

Bubba? The dogs know that name. The dogs love Bubba. They bark to say so.

A loud bell rings. We hear a voice over the PA system inside the school.

"That is the first bell. Children should be in their classrooms or going to their classrooms."

"The first bell? This is not going to according to the schedule." Mr. Zumwalt waves his clipboard. "There was no parade on the schedule." He turns to my mom. "These children have to stop marching and go to school."

"Good idea," says my mom. "Okeydokey, kids,

parade dismissed." My mom sticks her banner in the truck.

Mugsy tugs on Mr. Zumwalt's suit coat till he looks down.

"I just think you should know. I don't think I'm going to stay. But I'm checking it out for today."

"What?" asks Mr. Zumwalt. He checks his clipboard again.

I don't think Mugsy is on there. But someone should have warned him.

"I think I better take these poor babies for a little ride," Bubba says. "They get very upset when people are not friendly." He glares at Mr. Zumwalt. The dogs, who were happily wagging their tales a minute ago, all droop their heads, giving Bubba a sad look.

Another bell rings loudly.

"The schedule!" Mr. Zumwalt shouts as he runs to the school door.

"Nice to meet you," my mother calls after him.

"Conor, you okay? I'm going to walk Bella to her classroom."

"I know where I'm going, Mom," I tell her.

"Besides, he has Timmy and me to help him," Jack announces. "And I've got an extra eyeball."

"That makes me feel so much better," my mom answers.

Chapter Five

There Is Definitely Something Missing

Something is strange inside the school. I can tell. But even with my keen detective senses, I'm not sure exactly what it is.

The lobby looks the same. Brick walls, glass display cases, empty glass shelves, glass windows into the library, windows you can see through to the books inside. On one wall, a large framed picture of Edith R. Hammerrocker. She smiles down on us, one hand holding a book, the other hand reaching out, but hidden inside the frame of the picture.

The frame has always seemed interesting to me. It isn't gold, or fancy, or like any sort of frame you'd see around a picture in a museum. This one is made out different pieces of wood

banged together to make a frame around the picture. I once asked Mrs. Burton about it. She said, "It is just so Edith Hammerrocker."

Confusing.

And if Mrs. Roslyn Burton were here now, I could ask her what she meant. But she isn't.

Instead, we have a more-than-six-foot-tall jumping praying mantis.

I stop and look around me. What's wrong?

"What's wrong?" I ask my secret agent companions. After solving three different secret cases, surely they will know.

"Wrong?" Timmy asks.

The PA system sounds again. "All children should be in their classes by now."

"What's wrong is we're late. Time for a land-speed record for Not Running through the hall," Jack says.

He sets off at an impressive pace, feet flying while never technically breaking into a run.

We follow, turn down into a hall, and slide to a stop outside Mr. Lawal's room. Jack and Timmy hop into the classroom.

I stop.

Look at the door.

Look at the other doors.

Look down the hall.

And I see what's wrong. Or, to be exact, I don't see.

And that's what's wrong.

"Mr. Moloney, are you attending school this year?" Mr. Lawal calls from inside the classroom.

Which is where I go.

There's one empty desk in the room. With the name *Conor* on top. This top secret agent can figure anything out. I sit there.

"Now that Conor has decided to join us, I think we can begin the game. It is time for Batter Up! Time for the Big Kickoff. The Championship Tip-off. The puck is about to drop for the face-off."

Mr. Harlan "Lefty" Lawal was a baseball player before he was a teacher. He was a pretty good shortstop who played one major-league game and a lot of games in the minor leagues. As good a place as any to play ball, as he likes to tell us.

And now, every subject, everything he teaches, has to do with sports.

Every kid wants him for a teacher. Well, almost

every kid. Well, every kid who likes sports.

That would be me, Jack, Timmy, Mad Dog, and Murphy, for sure.

"First, I want you to call me Mr. Lefty. Second, on your desk is your box of school supplies. Let's begin by opening them up and marking our names in everything. Remember there is nothing worse than getting out on a field to play and finding you are wearing someone else's jersey."

We rip and tear the plastic around everything.

"I think we'll listen to a few inspirational thoughts as we do these simple chores. If your glove isn't oiled, you can't play well." Mr. Lefty pops a CD in the player.

Inspirational?

"Oh man, a lot of people singing at the same time," Jack worries.

"I don't see why kindergarten is the only grade where you get snacks," Timmy complains.

"Welcome to *A Sports Fan's Greatest Moments*,"

comes the voice from the machine. "Actual live broadcasts of those moments that people are talking about generations later."

Sweet.

And inspirational.

"Here we are at Yankee Stadium for game three of the 1927 World Series . . ."

Our class listens. We write our names, fill in the blanks, and watch Mr. Lefty walk around the room swinging an imaginary baseball bat. This is a great start to the new school year.

Except . . . except . . . something is still not right.

I wait till the cheers over Babe Ruth's home run die down.

"Mr. Lefty." I raise my hand.

"Yes, Conor?"

"Where's all your stuff?" I ask.

"Stuff?" he asks back.

"Yeah, all your cool stuff that is usually outside

your room? The net that makes the door into a hockey goal. And the painting on the windows that makes it look like kids are sitting in bleachers watching your class. And the goal posts on the wall next to the door, with footballs flying across it. And you're wearing a plain old white shirt, not the baseball shirt you usually wear." When you are a little kid at Hammerrocker, and Mr. Lefty is not your teacher, you walk by the door and wish you were walking into that classroom.

"Yeah, your stuff," says Jack.

"And what about that picture you usually have of Lucky Lucinda Lowery, the greatest woman baseball player?" Murphy remembers.

"And the giant container of popcorn in a stadium megaphone." Timmy sounds as if he wishes he could eat some right now. I see him pop a little purple something from underneath his desk chair and into his mouth.

Mr. Lefty doesn't answer us straightaway. He

looks at the sky. Or at the ceiling, which the sky is on the other side of. He swings the bat that isn't there a few more times.

"Sometimes in life, kids, the coach makes a call you don't agree with," Mr. Lefty explains. "But you have to say to yourself, 'He, or she, is the coach. He must know something I don't know.' Or, if you decide he is really wrong, then you have to go out and prove it. But there is no point in flying off the handle and jawing in a coach's face."

"Oh," I say.

"Huh?" Jack says.

"That doesn't sound fair," Murphy says.

"I don't know if it's fair," Mr. Lefty says, "but—"

He is interrupted by the voice of Mr. Zumwalt. "Will all the classes please come to the cafeteria for the opening day assembly? Remember to walk silently, single file, without a word," says the voice through the speaker in the wall.

"Without a word?" I ask.

"What time is lunch?" Timmy wants to know.

So we walk through the school single file, without a word. I see again what I saw before. Or what I didn't see. Which is anything up on the wall anywhere. Or on the doors or windows. The teachers at Hammerrrocker Elementary usually go crazy for the first day of school. Ducks, cowboys, pizzas, aliens, baseball players, pioneers—everything covers the walls. That's what's wrong. It feels weird, like we're in school when we're not supposed to be here.

We pass other classes walking silently, single file. Great. Let's change our name to the Edith R. Hammerrocker Zombies.

Chapter Six

So You Wanted to Change Your Name

The fifth-grade spirit squad is lined up in the front of the room waiting for us as we file into the cafeteria. There is a stage at one end of the room, big windows and a door at the other. The space in between is usually filled with tables. Right now, Molly McGuire, our custodian, finishes folding and wheeling the tables, pushing them off to one side.

The little kids are already there, sitting up front. I see Bella and Mugsy, side by side.

"Conor! Conor!" Bella waves.

I wave back this once. Tonight I will explain about how to act completely cool when you see your older brother in school.

All the classes are in. The teachers line up along the wall. And I see that all the teachers are wearing plain old white shirts. Of course Miss Karen the music teacher has on a big purple scarf and a lot of jewelry. But it still looks plain for her.

Miss Karen begins to pound the piano. The spirit squad does a cheer.

"School! There is nothing like it!
School! You want to try it!
School! You'll think it's cool!
You will dig the Golden Rule!
So don't be the fool
Who misses school!"

We are all clapping along. We shout out

"School" every time they get to the word. A little rocking going on.

Mugsy leaps up. And faces the crowd.

"But there is no pool! Here at this school!" she shouts out.

This gets her cheers and applause.

And Miss Gray rushing over to her.

"And there's a boy who drools! Here in this school!"

Bella stands up. "Conor, can I sing? You didn't tell me about singing!" she yells to the back.

I give her the big Sit Down, Don't Talk not-so-secret sign.

The music stops.

Miss Karen says, "Let's welcome our new principal to the school."

Mr. Alvino Zumwalt jumps into the room with a big smile on his face. His long arms shake brown-and-blue spirit squad pom-poms.

Kate B., the head of the spirit squad, yells:

"Everyone on your feet. Give me an H!"

"H!" we yell.

"Give me an A!"

"A!"

"Give me an M!"

"M!"

"Give me another M!"

"Another M!"

"Give me an E!'

"E!"

It goes on and on. It makes you wish your school was named the Sam School. Give me an S, an A, an M. Okay, we're done.

Kids have graduated before we have finished spelling *Hammerrocker*. Mr. Zumwalt's smile gets smaller and smaller with each letter.

"Thank you, thank you, kids," he says. "That was a most spirited and welcoming welcome. Oh, look here, this is no good." Mr. Zumwalt stops, leans over, and begins to pick up little pieces of paper that have fallen out of the pom-poms. He gets down on his hands and knees.

We all watch as he pushes the little pieces of paper into piles.

Then Miss Karen calls, "How about a Hammerrocker Hamsters Hello!"

"Hamsters! Hamsters!" we shout, give the finger-wiggling hello. "The Hammerrocker Hamsters welcome you!"

For a moment, there is silence.

Mr. Alvino "Zoot" Zumwalt gets slowly to his

feet. He stares at us. His mouth hangs open. His eyes are as wide as can be. He takes a step away, waving the microphone back and forth.

Like he is trying to erase us. Or like he's holding a sword to keep us away.

Kate B. looks at Miss Karen. "Should we do it again?" she asks.

"NO!" Mr. Zumwalt finally finds his words. "NO!"

He looks around, sees us staring at him. Shakes his whole body. Looks down at the microphone as if remembering where he is.

"No, thank you, I mean. That was . . . was enough. Now it is time to start this school year." Mr. Zumwalt calms down. "Yes, indeed, I am your new principal. I am the head of your school now. And we will have an exciting, exciting year full of big changes for all of us.

"Have you noticed how the school looks? I think we would all say it looks neat and—"

Crash!

Bang!

"Sorry, my bad." Molly McGuire, the custodian, dropped a table open during the last sentence.

"Neat and tidy. Neat and tidy. Clean walls and clean halls. Tidy hearts and tidy minds," Mr. Zumwalt singsongs the words, like a nursery rhyme.

I don't think I've heard that one in my house.

"I have two big and exciting announcements for you. The first is, I've decided to enter us into a contest for the Neatest School in America." Mr. Zumwalt looks at us as if he thinks we will jump up and down with the news. "Isn't that exciting?"

No one answers.

"This contest is sponsored by the company that makes Doesn't That Smell Clean?, which is a very fine cleaning product," Mr. Zumwalt explains. "For the next several days, I will make a videotape of our school to show how neat we are. We are going to be famous far and wide. And that's not all. There's more!"

Crash!

Bang!

"I'm so sorry, I don't know what's up with these tables," Molly McGuire shouts from across the room.

Mr. Zumwalt waves a piece of paper around with his long arm. He looks like a Bammerama bug that has caught the rare but tasty bush gnat.

"And the second announcment, students. Hear the names of the other schools in our district. And, *most important,* the names the students call themselves." He unfolds the paper. "The Wolfe Stars, the Brookline Beasts, the Kinkaid Falcons, the Bethpage Bulldogs, the Concord Cobras, the Stevenson Savages.

"Stars! Savages! Fierce, flying Falcons. These are names, boys and girls, names to wear with pride. And what are we called?"

Kate B. yells, "Hamsters!"

The spirit squad cheers, "Hamsters!"

A whole lot of the kids yell, "Yeah!"

Mr. Alvino Zumwalt yells, "No! No 'yeah'! Don't you see? The other schools have brave, strong names. You do not. You are named for a small rodent that gets lost in walls and does other not-good things."

The spirit squad yells, "Lost in walls!"

"No, 'lost in walls' is bad. Hamsters do not lead us to neatness, to greatness. I propose we have a new name. An exciting, new name for an exciting, new school."

New name? No more hamsters?

"I know," a voice yells. "Let's be the Sharks!"

"Yeah, Sharks!"

Let's see. Would those voices belong to Jeremiah, Jake, and Mick, by any chance? I look around and see large guys from Sylvan Glen yelling.

Oh yes, one fine secret agent sitting here.

"That would be no fair," Jack yells.

Mr. Zumwalt puts his hand to his ear, as if he cannot understand what he heard.

"Are we yelling? In assembly? Tsk, tsk."

Tsk, tsk?

"Excuse me, Mr. Principal Man," Jack yells. "That would be no fair."

"Sharks would be no fair?" Mr. Zumwalt asks.

"Yeah, no fair," Timmy adds. "The Sylvan Glen guys use the name *Sharks* for everything. It kinda belongs to them."

"How about Sting Rays?" someone shouts.

"Rattlesnakes are cool."

"Panthers!"

"Terminators!" a voice yells from up front. Mugsy.

"How about the Hammerrocker Hogs?" Timmy calls out.

There is silence for a moment.

"Did someone say the Hammerrocker Hogs?" Mr. Zumwalt asks.

"Hogs?" Jack looks at Timmy as if he has just turned into one.

"Yeah. Hogs," Timmy answers. "That way we keep the H. Besides, hogs always seem very happy to me."

"These are good suggestions." Mr. Zumwalt seems happy. "Well, mostly good suggestions. I'll think on them and pick one."

"You can't do that!"

"Excuse me?" Mr. Zumwalt does that very annoying hand-to-ear thing again. "I thought I just heard someone tell the new principal of the school, which would be me, that I could not do something. Who would speak to me this way?"

Chapter Seven

Speak Up, Hamster Man

"My brother said you could not do that," Bella announces from up front.

Mugsy shouts from her seat between two teachers, "Do you want me to get him, Conor?"

"Conor? Who is Conor?" asks Mr. Zumwalt.

"He's over there," Jeremiah shouts. Helpful guy.

"Why don't you stand and explain to me why I cannot do what I want."

"You are so in trouble," Jack says in a helpful voice.

"Here." Timmy slips a candy in my hand. It's a little sticky.

I stand up. Which makes me feel oh so tall when everyone else is sitting on the floor.

"It doesn't seem fair to me that you should pick a name for everyone," I tell him. "I mean, it's our school. I think we should pick."

"Your school?" Mr. Zumwalt asks. "I believe that I am in charge. Which, I think, would make it my school."

Bang!

Crash!

"I'll call maintenance to send someone over to look at these tables," Molly McGuire says as another one falls.

"I think it is your school if you're the principal," I agree. "But isn't it your school if you're a teacher? Or a student, or anything? And if it's everyone's school, then on big stuff like this, everyone should vote."

"Vote! Vote!" the kids chant. Well, Jack and

Timmy and Bella and Mugsy and Murphy and Mad Dog.

But they get it started.

"Vote."

"Vote," comes a voice from the line of teachers.

Well, all right, Mr. Lefty.

"And I like the name Hamsters," I add, since I'm probably already in such big trouble with Mr. Zoot Zumwalt that I'll never leave this school until I'm forty-seven years old. "Hammerrocker Hamsters is a good name, and I don't want to change it."

"Hamsters!"

"Sharks!"

"Panthers!"

"Quiet!" Mr. Zumwalt yells. "No yelling."

Mr. Lefty stands up, holds up two fingers, giving a V sign.

We all give it back to him. And stop talking.

"So," Mr. Zumwalt says. "We will vote. One week from today, here in assembly. Those of you with opinions have seven days to convince the other students."

He swings his head back and forth, looking carefully at the room. "Who will be in charge of the Shark vote?"

Jeremiah waves his hand and is chosen.

"Panthers?"

Gavin gets to lead the Vote for Panthers group, and Matthew gets to be the Sting Ray man.

"Well done, students and teachers. Hasn't this been an awesome first assembly? And a great start to a new, neat-and-clean school year." Mr. Zumwalt picks up his clipboard. I can tell he is going to dismiss us.

"You forgot Hamsters," I call out. "You forgot to put someone in charge of the Hamster vote."

"I thought we were trying to replace that name," Mr. Zumwalt says.

"I thought we were trying to choose," I answer. "Maybe we choose to stay the same."

"No one would be called a Hamster by choice." Mr. Zumwalt does that microphone-waving thing again.

"That's what the vote will show," calls Molly McGuire.

Mr. Zumwalt stares at her. Stares at me. Waves his arms up and down.

"Are you telling me that you want to try to convince a whole school of forward-looking, tidy students and teachers that they should continue to call themselves Hamsters?"

If you put it that way . . .

"Yes, I want to try."

Mr. Zumwalt says quietly, "We'll see if you can."

Then loudly, "Assembly is dismissed!"

We line up by class.

Bella calls out "Bye, Conor! Bye!"

I hear Mugsy asking loudly, "Who was that guy?"

"What's for lunch today?" Timmy asks.

Good questions.

Chapter Eight

Genghis Khan and Bob

The first day of school is over. And I'm now called Hamster Man by a lot of kids I don't like anyway.

"Congratulations, Conor." Jack shakes my hand as we walk home from school. "That was an amazing land-speed record. You made the new principal hate you in the first hour of school."

I shake my head. "I am in such big trouble."

"Have a lollipop," Timmy says. "It will help."

"Is it still wrapped?" I ask.

"Yup." Timmy produces one from his pocket.

"Has it been unwrapped before?" I check the important facts.

"And have you ever given it to Riley?" Jack asks.

"I can't remember," Timmy answers.

"Uh, no thanks."

"Okay." Timmy pops it into his mouth.

"I'm going to make posters to put up at school," I tell them. "Can you guys help?"

"I'll be there." Timmy salutes.

"I'll be there first," Jack promises.

"I'll bring something," Timmy says.

"I'll come," Bella says.

"Me too. I have some good ideas," Mugsy says. "But we'll need a whole lot of sticks. And black paint."

A short while later I sit in The Secret Place, surrounded by open books, piles of writing paper, markers, and poster-size paper.

I've printed out lots of information from the computer, from a site called www.hamstersare heaven.com.

The guy who runs this Web site sure loves hamsters. Especially his hamsters, Betty and

Dan. He does seem to know everything there is to know about them. Although I wonder how he found out about Baby, Genghis Khan's hamster.

And my mom drew a few pictures to put on the posters.

I tape a big piece of paper to the wall. It reads IMPORTANT FACTS ABOUT HAMSTERS.

Which might help.

And at least Bella and Mugsy have to go to ballet class this afternoon. So I can avoid their help.

"Help," cries a voice as the person who uses it crashes into the room. "Help?" I ask Jack as he peels himself off the wall opposite the door. A little too much land speed.

"I'm here to help," he announces. Fingers snapping, legs jiggling, Jack gets down to work.

"Okay, what are we doing? How many posters do we have to make? Is this like homework? Are we sure we want to do this? Has the principal called your mom yet? Is this going to be any fun?

Will we be finished by the time *Race Boy* comes on? I hate to miss even one episode."

I'm trying to decide which question to answer when the door crashes open. Again.

Timmy falls into the room. Holding some kind of glass box in his hand. Which he manages to keep upright as he rolls forward.

Impressive.

"It's hard to open the door and hold this at the same time," he explains.

"Knocking works," I inform him.

"What is that?" Jack asks. "Why did you bring it? Why don't I know about it?"

"It's Bob."

"Bob?"

"Bob?"

I always worry when Jack and I think the same thoughts.

"Bob the hamster." Timmy puts the case down on the floor. "I brought him to help."

"Is he good at drawing posters?" I ask.

"Hamsters can draw?" Jack asks.

"I haven't asked him," Timmy answers. "But Russell next door had to get rid of him because he's moving to Africa. So I thought we could keep him in The Secret Place."

"Because?" I ask.

"Because it would be good inspiration," Timmy answers. "Look how cute he is."

Bob looks out at us from his little hamster world. I see a pointy hamster nose, a long hamster tail, and black hamster eyes.

Little hamster eyes that get wider. Little hamster paws that fly up into the air. A little hamster body that runs into the tunnel thing.

"What's wrong with Bob?" Timmy asks.

"He thinks he's about to die," Jack answers.

Riley has decided to come see what's going on. She circles the cage, sniffs, circles, whines, sniffs, circles. Barks a loud hello.

Bob pulls his tail into the tunnel, trying to disappear.

"Do dogs eat hamsters?" Timmy asks.

"Riley tries to eat *my* flesh," Jack insists. "Why not a hamster too?"

Bob sticks his head out to see what is going on.

Riley barks again.

Bob faints.

"Tell me again," Jack asks, "why you think we should keep the name *Hamster*?"

"Poor Bob." Timmy taps on the glass. "Do you think we should give him a gumdrop or something?"

"I don't know, Timmy," I tell the truth. "I don't even know if we can keep him here. But right now we've got to make some posters."

"Let's roll," Timmy answers.

"Don't we have to make the posters before we roll them?" Jack wonders.

After dinner I come out to The Secret Place to clean up from the poster making. And to check on Bob. He seems happy enough. Sitting in his cage, he throws the little wood stuff up into the air. Maybe he's celebrating Hamsters' New Year. Or the fact that Riley is in the house and not sticking her nose against the cage. Bob the hamster celebrates the defeat of the giant hairy black monster.

My mom said she is not sure about a hamster. Gave me the old "We'll see."

Which usually means, "No, but I'll tell you that later."

We'll see, I guess.

I pick up the Book, the real and true Secret Files of the Freaky Joe Club. Now and again I like to sit and read the old cases. I like to memorize the rules.

And besides, I can't help it. I think there is something funny going on here. I mean, what is the big deal about us being called the Hamsters? Why does that bother Zoot Zumwalt so much? Why does he need to change our name right away?

I think there is a mystery here. If I knew why it was such a big deal to change it, it might be easier to fight back.

And why do I care so much about the name *Hamsters*? That's another mystery.

Okay, it's not the same as a whole joust disappearing.

But as Chuck would say to Sir Chester, "Gadzooks. Something doth smell wrong."

Maybe a dip into the Secret Files will help.

I begin to unlock the bicycle chain.

And Bob begins to go crazy. Stops his party. Jumps up and down. Makes hamster noises.

"What's up, buddy?" I ask.

Bob answers me by running in circles.

"Conor! You have to come in!" Bella calls loudly from outside the door.

"Okay!" I yell from inside the door.

She leaves.

Bob calms down the way Riley does after she has done her Someone Is Coming barking.

Interesting.

It's something else that I need to investigate further. I tape a useful piece of paper to the wall.

Things to Figure Out

1. Why does Mr. Zumwalt want to change our name?
2. Why did they pick the name "Hamster" anyway?
3. Does Bob have hidden hamster talents?

Bob begins to run around in circles, jump up and down, and wave his tail wildly.

"Conor!"

Very, very interesting. Is Bob a psychic hamster?

"Keep an eye on them, Bob," I tell him as I put the Secret Files carefully down.

Bob moves his little hamster arms.

Gadzooks.

Did he just salute?

Chapter Nine

What About Christopher Columbus?

"Ay kink ye hmm pot um umhum hmmm hor."

"What?" Jack and Timmy ask at the same time.

I take the roll of tape out of my mouth.

"I think we should put a poster over here."

"Maybe we should put our posters where they do," Timmy suggests. He points to Jeremiah and Jake, who are hanging a poster next to the front door.

A giant silver shark with giant silver teeth seems to leap off the giant silver poster. The glittering silver words read:

SHARKS RULE THE OCEAN! SHARKS WILL RULE THE SCHOOLS! VOTE FOR A WINNER! THE KIND THAT CAN EAT YOU FOR DINNER!

"Later, Hamster Man," Jeremiah calls as they head off with what look like two more big and— I hate to say it—*cool* posters.

"I might have to vote for them," Jack says.

"Let's put mine by the library. And Timmy's by the cafeteria."

Jack and Timmy hold mine up. I tape. We stand back to look.

A hamster dressed like Abraham Lincoln smiles at us. He holds a scroll with the words:

BE TRUE TO YOUR SCHOOL.
HAMSTERS WE HAVE ALWAYS BEEN.
HAMSTERS WE SHOULD ALWAYS BE.
VOTE HAMSTER!

"It sounded better yesterday," I admit.

Timmy's poster works by the cafeteria. A picture of a hamster with his cheeks puffed up, full of food, with the words:

WOULDN'T YOU
WANT TO BE THIS
GUY'S FRIEND?
VOTE HAMSTER.

We catch up with the Sharks team

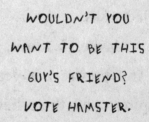

and the Sting Rays outside the gym. Fierce underwater creatures face each other from posters on opposite walls.

"This is the perfect place for my poster," Jack points out. "You guys were so wrong about my idea."

A very large vampire hamster wears a long cape and bares his giant, bloody hamster fangs. The words HORRIBLE HAMSTERS HAUNT HAMMER-ROCKER are written as though they were dripping red blood.

"Now aren't you glad I didn't listen to you?" Jack asks.

"Maybe," I admit. "But hamsters are not big. And they're not generally known to be vampires. And there have also been no reports of them haunting the school."

"Okay, but besides that?" Jack asks.

The sound of a basketball bouncing our way saves me from having to answer.

Mrs. Stern, the gym teacher, and our own Mr. Lefty come tearing around the corner, passing the ball between them.

"Whoa, Maggie, look, student people," Mr. Lefty says as he almost runs into us.

He and Mrs. Stern check out our posters.

"Very cool," they both agree. "Oh. But—" they both say at the same time.

"What are these doing here?" Mr. Zumwalt yells before they can finish. He comes around the same corner, his hands full of posters with the tape hanging off of them. He balances a video camera under his arm.

"They are not supposed to be here," I explain.

"They are supposed to be on the wall," Timmy adds.

"Now we have to put them up again," Jack tells him.

"They are not supposed to be on the wall! The walls are supposed to be clean! Clean and neat and tidy. So we can win the neatest-school-in-the-country award. Neat school, new name."

I have to say that the vocabulary word to describe Mr. Zumwalt right now would be *upset*.

"But they're neat posters," Timmy points out.

"And how can we get kids to vote otherwise?" I add. "Posters are a traditional tool of elections. To help voters decide."

"Huh?" says Jake.

"You read that in a book, didn't you?" Jack asks.

"No posters!" Mr. Zumwalt says. "No posters!" Like we didn't hear him the first time. "Put them in a neat pile somewhere and take them home with you."

"But—"

"But—"

"No buts. Away with them. I am now going to finish my daily video of our neat school. I'll do the gym now and then retrace my steps. To show the walls without posters."

"Let me help you guys with this." Mr. Lefty helps us sort out Hamster posters from Shark ones. "Don't worry, we'll figure something out."

"How can the kids vote if they don't know what they're voting for?" I ask.

"Good question," Mr. Lefty agrees.

Mr. Zumwalt does not appear to hear us as he fusses with his camera. "Wide angle lens for the whole beautiful, shiny wood floor of the gym," he says, mostly to himself.

"Let me get that for you, Mr. Z." Mrs. Stern holds the door to the gym open.

"Greetings again to everyone at the Doesn't That Smell Clean? Company," Mr. Zumwalt speaks loudly to the video camera. "Here on day two of the contest, I am entering the gym of Edith Hammerrocker Elementary. I think you can see, as I can, that the gym is—What in the name of Christopher Columbus is going on?"

Huh?

Chapter Ten

That's a Lotta Hamsters

"Now that is something you don't see every day," Mr. Lefty says.

"Uh, yeah," Mrs. Stern agrees.

We push past Mr. Zumwalt, who has stopped speaking loudly. I would tell him he might want to close his mouth, which is hanging open. But I figure I'm not the one he wants to hear it from.

And I'm a bit distracted by something you don't see every day.

The gym is filled with, um, well, sort of creatures. Creatures made from brown grocery bags. And paper, and well, all sorts of stuff. They all have pointy ears, and pointy noses, and long tails that look to be made out of jump ropes.

Whoever made them would not be in the running for Artist of the Week in Miss Forte's art class.

But whoever made these made a lot of them. They are marching across the floor, climbing up all the ropes, walking across the balance beam. One is standing on the vault. Another sits in the basketball hoop.

These brown bag creatures fill the gym.

"I wonder who did that?" Jeremiah says.

"Yeah," says Jake.

"What are they?" Matthew asks.

"You *do* know what they look like, don't you?" Timmy whispers to me.

I look again. Oh boy.

"You know what they look like?" Jack says.

"What?" asks Mr. Lefty.

"Oh, they do," Mrs. Stern says.

"Wow," Jeremiah says.

"They're hamsters!" Jack announces triumphantly.

"Who would do this?" Mr. Zumwalt asks in a horrified voice.

"I usually end up thinking it's Conor," Jacks adds helpfully.

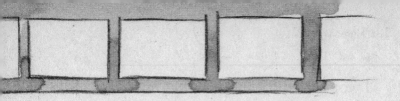

"Jack!" I come close to shouting.

"Conor?" Mr. Zumwalt says.

"It would be important to know that Jack is almost always completely wrong about almost everything," Timmy says.

"I wonder how it jumped that high?" Jack says. He pretends to dribble. "He drives down the lane. He shifts—he turns—he shoots—he scores! That's one Hamster scored for the home team."

"End zone dance," Timmy cries. He and Jack dance, each one with a hamster.

Miss Karen rushes into the gym. She stops to look with her mouth open. "Mr. Zumwalt," she calls. "What are we supposed to do with the note in all our classrooms?"

"Classrooms?" Mr. Zumwalt turns on his heel and runs his Bammerama-bug run out of the gym.

Mr. Lefty follows him.

Mrs. Stern starts to lower the climbing rope to bring one hamster down.

I follow Mr. Lefty.

Something is going on here.

I catch up to them outside Mr. Lefty's classroom, which happens to be the one closest to the gym.

"That wasn't there when I left last night," Mr. Lefty says.

"And did you write that?" Mr. Zumwalt asks, his long arm pointing to the blackboard.

"Nope," Mr. Lefty says. "Not my error."

Mr. Zumwalt runs from the room to the next classroom. Mr. Lefty follows. I do too.

Same words.

Every classroom.

A bell rings.

The PA system calls out, "Mr. Zumwalt, the students are arriving. Mr. Zumwalt."

"Students? Students?" Mr. Zumwalt begins to turn in circles, flapping his wings. I mean, arms. "We can't have students here today."

"I'm afraid we don't have a vote on that one, Mr. Zumwalt." Mr. Lefty picks up an eraser. "I'll get this one for you."

"Good. Good. I'll send the students to the gym," Mr. Zumwalt says. "No! I can't send them there. I'll send them to the cafeteria. Call the teachers to the gym. Yes. That's it. I'm in charge, I'm in charge."

He runs out.

"Well, whattaya know?" Mr. Lefty does that kind of half laugh, half spit thing.

"I don't know anything, I didn't do this," I swear.

"Ah, don't worry, Conor, it's okay."

I help Mr. Lefty erase the words. But I'm not sure it's okay. What I am sure of is that I'm somehow going to get in trouble for this.

Written on every blackboard in the school are the words:

On that fateful day,
a hamster was the answer.

Knowing the answer is good, I guess. But it would be better to know the question.

And much better not to be the one called Hamster Man.

Chapter Eleven

Spotted Moms and People in Glass Cages

"Everyone listen to me! This is your principal!" Mr. Zumwalt's excited voice comes through the speaker box in the wall. "All students will report to the cafeteria. All teachers go now to the gym."

"Oh, that'll work," Mr. Lefty says.

"Huh?"

"Just who will be in charge in the cafeteria, Hamster Man?" Mr. Lefty asks.

Good point.

"I gotta go," I tell him.

"See you in the on-deck circle."

When I get to the cafeteria, no one is in charge.

In the front, Mugsy is teaching some kids to crawl across the floor on elbows and knees. Bella and some others are doing something that looks like ballet.

In the middle, a fair amount of kids are hitting one another with backpacks.

In the back, it looks like a group of Sharks are attacking some Sting Rays.

A loud whine fills the room.

With her guitar around her neck, Molly McGuire fusses with the microphone till it stops whining.

"That'll do. Everyone sit down. Everyone stop hitting anyone near you. I do not feel like mopping up blood today."

She waits.

"Unless you feel like helping me clean all the bathrooms, I suggest you cool it now," Molly tells us.

That works.

"Here's a song about our very own city. I'll sing one line, and you repeat." She hums, strums a little, and begins.

"Oh, first the sky was clear on that awful day."

Not much singing back.

"I will give the teachers the names of everyone who doesn't sing. For extra homework," Molly suggests.

"Oh, first the sky was clear on that awful day."

We sing it loudly back.

"What was to come, oh none could say.
All could have been lost,
Yes, everyone's home,
By the terrible rains
From the heavenly dome,
But for one person,
Whose brave tale I will now tell,
Who with her buddy did sound
The warning bell."

Someone should have sounded a warning bell about Mr. Zumwalt. He interrupts the song in the middle of a line.

"Oh, Ead . . ."

"Oh, Ead," we sing.

Ead? This is a song about burping Matthew Eads?

"Students! Students! Pay attention to me. Something is wrong in our school." Mr. Zumwalt puts his arms high and wide.

He has everyone's attention.

"Someone has been writing on the blackboards."

"Oh no, writing on blackboards. That has to stop." Jeremiah says it just loud enough for us to hear him.

Which gets a good laugh.

Which clearly annoys our principal. Who is not in a good mood.

"And someone has filled the gym with a great deal of rubbish. Rubbish in the shape of hamsters. Hamster rubbish that will take a great deal of time to clean up. So there will be no gym today for any of the grades."

This causes a loud, unhappy noise to rise up in the cafeteria.

He goes on. "This is not acceptable. This is not tidy. This will not win us a prize for the neatest school. Everyone go to your classrooms now. And you will use your gym period to write a composition beginning with the words: *I love to be clean because . . .*"

Everyone moans. Many, many people look at me.

Mr. Zumwalt finishes with asking, "If anyone wishes to take responsibility for this, please see me."

No one confesses.

Which may be why I find myself outside Mr. Zumwalt's office after school. Waiting for my mother.

With Jack and Timmy, who want to know
what is going on. And Bella, who has to walk
home with me. And Mugsy, who is supposed to
come to our house after school.

"Why did you do it, Conor?" Jack asks. "When
did you do it? How did you get the hamster in the
basketball hoop? I didn't think they bounced."

"I didn't do it, Jack," I tell him.

"No?"

"Then why did he call your mom?" Timmy asks.

"Good question," I answer.

"Good question," my mom agrees as she races
through the door with Mugsy's little brother,
Mikey, and his best buddy, Dwayne, in tow. "I'm
watching them," she explains.

"We were painting with her," Mikey says.

"Big bugs," Dwayne adds.

Which would be why they are covered in purple
and yellow paint?

"Kids, everyone sit here on the bench quietly, and do nothing. Timmy and Jack, you are in charge. Conor, let's go."

So I go to face my doom with my purple-, yellow-, and green-spotted mother. Who thinks that Jack and Timmy can be in charge of Bella, Mugsy, Mikey, and Dwayne.

Oh boy.

"So you see, Mrs. Moloney, why I had to call you," Mr. Zumwalt finishes his long story. "Posters on the wall of my school. Writing on every blackboard. A gym full of giant hamsters. Something must be done."

"Surely something must be done," my mom agrees.

Mom?

"How can Conor and I help you?" she asks.

"Huh?" Mr. Zumwalt says.

"I'm not sure how, but we will surely do anything to help our wonderful school." My mom turns to me. "Conor, do you have any suggestions?"

"No."

"I don't either, but I'm sure something will come to me. I'll get back to you as soon as possible, Mr. Zumwalt."

"Mrs. Moloney, I don't think you understand. Something must be done about your son's behavior." Mr. Zumwalt picks up a pencil and bangs it on the table.

"Conor's behavior? What's wrong with Conor's behavior?"

"He put posters up on the walls of my school!" Mr. Zumwalt explains.

"That is traditional in an election," my mother points out.

"That's what he said. But no posters are allowed on the walls of my school," Mr. Zumwalt says.

"Conor, do you understand, no posters?" Mom asks.

"I do now," I tell her.

"Good. What else, Mr. Zumwalt?"

Mr. Zumwalt stares at her.

"Mr. Zumwalt, I don't mean to be rude, but I have small children waiting in the lobby, and I'm sure you must have a lot of meetings scheduled, so is there anything else?"

I like spotted moms.

"Meetings? Scheduled?" Mr. Zumwalt looks confused.

"With the other parents of children who put posters up on your wall. Surely Conor was not the only one?" My mom smiles at him.

"Mrs. Moloney, there was a whole gym filled to the brim with unattractive, large, scary hamsters. And someone wrote a note about hamsters on all the blackboards." Mr. Zumwalt bangs the pencil with almost every word.

"And?" my mom asks.

"And your son is leading
the campaign to keep the name
Hamsters!" Mr. Zumwalt finishes.

"And what has that got to do with the other
things?"

"That's what I want to know!" I think the new
vocabulary word for Mr. Zumwalt is *frustrated*.

"Conor, do you know who made the hamsters

and put them in the gym? Or wrote on the blackboards?"

I tell the truth. "No, I don't."

"I'm afraid I don't know either," Mom tells him. She stands up and shakes his hand. "Sorry we couldn't help you."

Before Mr. Zumwalt can answer, there is a light tapping at the door.

"Conor's mom, Conor's mom," Timmy whispers through the door. "I think you should come."

Uh-oh.

"Uh-oh," Mom says.

We run.

"How did they get in there?" Mom wants to know.

Mikey, Dwayne, and Mugsy are crammed into the display case in the lobby. The one for library books.

Jack is trying to open the door.

"You guys have to lean back, not on the door,"
he shouts at them.

"I want to get out!" Mikey yells.

"I'm squished," Dwayne cries.

"I'm a man-eating tiger," Mugsy growls.

"I'm not happy," my mom tells everyone. "Go
get Molly, Conor."

I find Molly McGuire.

She brings her tools.

Jack and Timmy hold the glass on each side while my mom and Molly use the tools.

Bella does a dance for them while they work.

Mr. Zumwalt walks out with his video camera. Looks. Goes back to his office.

"I've almost got it," Molly tells my mom. She leans back, bumping into the picture of Edith R. Hammerrocker.

"Hold on one sec. Conor, help me take the picture down. I don't want to send her flying by mistake."

Molly and I lift Edith off the wall. The frame isn't heavy like I thought it would be. Up so close, I can see that the whole frame is made of driftwood. The whirls and twirls in the wood were made by water. Why frame a school portrait with wood like that? Could this mean something?

"Okay, slide it over gently, guys." Molly and my mom move the door over. And free the animals from the display case.

"I am never, ever going to do what Mugsy says again," Mikey swears.

"Here you go, little guys," Timmy says as he hands them something in a color I've never seen before.

"Let's lock this baby back up," Molly says.

"It was locked," Jack explains. "But Mugsy opened the door."

"It was nothing," Mugsy says.

As I go to put the picture back, I notice it is a little loose in the frame. I wiggle it a little. It slides a little bit to one side. I can see Edith's hand, the one that is usually hidden. And what is in her hand!

Oh boy.

"Look at all the big trucks," Bella says.

"Who called the fire department?" Jack asks.

"Police cars!" Dwayne yells. "I love police cars."

"Oh boy," my mom says.

Chapter Twelve

The Smart Guys Meet Vasco da Gama

"I thought for sure they would arrest us," Jack says. "Or at least Mugsy."

"Do they feed you in jail?" Timmy wonders.

"I think they should have taken Mugsy," Jack adds. "I mean, she's more guilty than anyone who helped her climb in."

"Mr. Zumwalt says he called the fire department to rescue the kids and the police answered the same call," I remind them.

At least that's what he said.

It was fun listening to Mr. Zumwalt explain to the policeman that he didn't have missing property. He had property he didn't want. Hamsters that didn't belong to him.

"I'd have liked to ride in the police car. To see

how fast they go." Jack taps on Bob's glass.
"Hello, little Bob."

Bob moves his arms.

"Whoa, Bob just waved at me. He likes me.
Hamsters are so much smarter than dogs." Jack
sticks his nose on the glass.

Bob spits at him.

"Conor, why did you say we
had to have a meeting?" Timmy asks. "I've
still got to do my hockey fractions. 'If Ray
Borque played twenty-two seasons, and won
one Stanley Cup, what percentage . . .'"

"Timmy, we have to get organized for our new case. Secret File Number Four." I tape a piece of paper to the wall.

"Not the paper," Jack cries.

"What case?" Timmy asks.

"That's a good question," I answer. "We might have more than one mystery."

"I don't think he spit at me; I think he's drooling," Jack says.

I write:

1. Why is it so important for Mr. Zumwalt to change our name from the Hammerrocker Hamsters?

"Because he is the Weird Principal," Timmy suggests.

"Because he never met Bob," Jack says. "Bob who likes everyone."

Bob bares his teeth at Jack.

"Look, he's smiling at me,"
Jack insists.

I write some more:

2. Who put hamsters
   in the gym and wrote on all the
   blackboards? And what did that
   message mean?

"What was the message again?" Timmy asks.
"It was erased before we got there."

"'On that fateful day, a hamster was the
answer,'" I recite.

"What day are they talking about?" Jack
asks. His fingers begin to snap. "And what was
the question? That would be important to
know."

"You know, it would be interesting to know
which hamster we're talking about," Timmy suggests.

"Good points," I agree.

"'Cause we are the Smart Guys," Jack says.

"Which brings me to a very interesting fact I learned today." I pause for a moment to show that this is important.

"Which is?" Timmy and Jack both ask.

"In her school picture, Edith R. Hammerrocker is holding a hamster. It is hidden by the frame," I announce.

"So?" Jack asks.

"Why is it hidden? Why a hamster?" I ask.

"Maybe the picture was simply too big for the frame," Timmy suggests. "My mom has a picture of her family that leaves out my uncle Donald."

"And because her school nickname is the *Hamsters*," Jack snaps his fingers as he thinks, "the painter put a hamster in the picture."

"Oh." That could be the answer. But then it's not much of a mystery.

"Of course, they do call him Strange Uncle Donald," Timmy adds.

"Just ask us your important questions," Jack says. "And the Smart Guys will answer."

This is scary. It looks like Jack is right.

"You still have two other mysteries," Timmy tells me.

And Timmy is also right.

"Who made all those hamsters? And put them in the gym? And why?" I only know it wasn't me.

"Both your mysteries have to do with hamsters," Jack points out.

"That's good thinking, Jack," Timmy says.

"It is a good thing the Jack Man is here today."

"What can that tell us?" I ask. Jack is clearly on a roll.

"I think . . . I think . . ." Jack walks slowly in a circle, his hand under his chin, thinking big Jack thoughts. "I think . . . Bob did it!"

"Bob?" I ask.

"Let me get this straight, Jack," Timmy says. "Bob broke out of his cage, made a whole bunch of hamsters out of grocery bags, took them up to the gym, wrote on all the blackboards, painted himself into a picture, came home, and still had enough energy to spit on you."

"That about sums it up."

"He's some hamster."

"I've been trying to tell you that," Jack says.

Bob starts his running and jumping act.

Riley barks.

My mom sticks her head in the door.

"What are you guys up to?"

"Oh, nothing," Jack answers.

"Not a good answer, Jack. Time to go, fellas. And remember, you promised to help out at Mugsy's birthday party on Saturday."

"Mom?" I start to complain.

"No complaints, no cries of pain, nothing. You

all agreed," she reminds us. "And you had fun helping at Bella's party."

"But Bella's party was a skating party," I point out. "What is Mugsy doing?"

"I don't know," my mom admits. "I'll go call her mom."

"There'll be cake, won't there?" Timmy asks.

"Mom, can you walk Bella to school?" I ask in the morning. "I want to go to the library before school starts."

"That'll work," she tells me.

"Did you call Mrs. Magoolaghan to find out about the party?"

"I'll do it today," Mom promises.

As I slip into the library, I see Mr. Zumwalt heading down the hall, talking to his video camera.

Miss Hoopes, the librarian, is in her office.

"You're early," she notices.

"I need your help," I tell her.

"That's music to a librarian's ear," she says with a smile. "Throw your question at me."

"How can I find out why the school was named for Edith Hammerrocker?"

"Ooh, I like this one." Miss Hoopes rubs her hands together. "I think we can do it right here on the computer." Miss Hoopes starts clicking away like mad on the keyboard.

"School system Web site. Elementary school page. School names. And bingo."

"Bingo?"

"Under history of the names: Edith R. Hammerrocker was a brave librarian who worked for thirty-five years in our school system. As she both enriched and saved the lives of so many children of our fair city, it is a privilege and an honor to name this new school the Edith R. Hammerrocker Elementary School."

"Interesting," I say.

"Very," Miss Hoopes says.

"Brave," I read.

"Doesn't that just sound like a librarian?" Miss Hoopes smiles.

"But what's this about saving lives?" I wonder.

"Never underestimate the power of a book, Conor."

"I wish I knew more."

"Well, then let's head to the stacks. 'Always rely on the books' is my motto." Miss Hoopes heads out into the library.

I follow.

"I just love this book," Miss Hoopes says as she pulls off the shelf a big, thick, gray-green book with yellow pages. "*A History of Prater County from Then Till Now.*"

"That's us," I realize.

"Index first." Miss Hoopes balances the book on her arm, turning to the back. "G, H, here it is, Hammerrocker. Page three hundred forty-seven."

"Holy moly!"

Miss Hoopes and I look at each other.

"Ow!"

"What in the name of Vasco da Gama is going on here?"

Miss Hoopes and I run into the main part of the library.

Principal Zumwalt lies on the floor on top of a pile of books, his video camera aimed at the ceiling. And there are more books in piles all around him.

"Are you okay?" Miss Hoopes asks.

"No, I am not okay. I am on the floor. In the middle of a mess!" Mr. Zumwalt gets slowly to his feet, wobbling a little.

At that moment Molly McGuire and Mr. Lefty come in together.

"Whoa, big mess," Mr. Lefty says.

"Interesting mess," Molly says. "Look at the piles."

We all stare. I see what she means.

Oh boy.

Miss Hoopes sees. "Goodness me. Someone went to some trouble to make the books spell a letter. See, two piles side by side with a tall book across the middle. The letter H."

I count six big piles, all in the shape of the letter H.

Molly McGuire slides one of the long books out. "I knew it. *Madeline.*"

"Oh, those are always too tall for the shelves." Miss Hoopes smiles.

"*Madeline?*" Mr. Zumwalt does not seem interested in an old house in Paris. "How did this mess get here, is what I want to know. Why did someone use books to spell the letter H? For what?"

"*Hammerrocker?*" Miss Hoopes thinks out loud. "Or *Hamster?*"

Mr. Zumwalt notices me. "Conor? "Why are you here?"

"I was helping Conor with some research when we heard you crash," Miss Hoopes answers for me.

"Interesting," Mr. Zumwalt says.

Uh-oh.

"The important thing is to get this cleaned up," Miss Hoopes says. "Molly, would you get me a passel of fifth graders?"

"Clean, yes, tidy it up," Mr. Zumwalt says.

Pulling my arm, Mr. Lefty says, "Conor, let's hit the road."

Good idea.

A passel of fifth graders quickly spreads the word. Mysterious piles of the letter H are found in the library. And H is the first letter of *Hamster*. Hamsters were found in the gym yesterday. Hamsters made everyone write a silly essay. And Conor is the Hamster Man.

I spend lunchtime and recess saying, "No, I didn't do it."

"You know, Conor, making books spell the letter H might be a good idea," Jack says. "But only if you put it where kids could see it."

"But I didn't do it," I remind him.

"Look at these flyers," Timmy says.

He hands me a silver piece of paper.

SHARKS, SHARKS, SHARKS.
MEANEST THINGS IN THE SEA.
EXACTLY WHAT WE OUGHT TO BE. VOTE SHARKS.

"We can make flyers tomorrow," I promise.

After lunch, the voice of Zumwalt speaks to us.

"I have found silver pieces of paper on the floor of my school. Will Conor Moloney, Matthew Eads, and the other team leaders report to my office immediately."

The whole class salutes me as I leave. Why do I have the terrible feeling they think I'm not coming back?

"Students in my school," Mr. Zumwalt says to us as we line up in his office. "How can we win an award for the neatest school when there is paper dropped on the floor?"

None of us answers.

"This has to stop. No more paper. On Tuesday we will have an assembly. Each one of you will tell your fellow students why they should vote for your idea. Then we will vote. And our school will then have a new mascot. And this business will be over."

Mr. Zumwalt leans down over all of us. "No more paper."

I decide not to point out that we might still have an old mascot.

And I forget to ask Matthew Eads why he was in Molly's song.

Chapter Thirteen

A Search and Destroy Mission

After school, I finally get a minute to finish *The Secret of the Mysterious Disappearing Joust*. No fellow secret agents, no little sister turning flip-flops, no students making Hamster jokes to bother me.

In chapter thirteen, Chuck is speaking to Sir Chester.

"Sire, I doth repeat the words again. We must find the Guanyuian Book of Spells, if we shallst stop this evil."

The book! In all the fuss, I forgot.

A History of Prater County from Then Till Now. Page number . . . what? I forget. Edith's name was there. And I was about to learn something important, I'm sure of it.

I'll head up to school.

And if Molly is there, I can ask her why we were singing a song about Matthew.

I leave my bicycle by the front door.

Which is unlocked. Which is good.

"Hello?" I call.

No answer.

"You can go to the library and see if Miss Hoopes is there," my mom said when I asked. "Then come straight home."

I go to the library. The door opens.

"Hello?"

No one home. But the book must still be here.

It's not on the shelf where it was today.

And it's not on the checkout desk. Dang.

Think, Conor.

I head to the back where Mr. Zumwalt hit the floor.

And there it is on the table where Miss Hoopes
put it down.

I open to the index in the back. Wrong letter.
Too far back in the alphabet.

My eyes slide down the page.

Whoa.

Now there's a name I know.

Page 532. That I have to see.

What was that noise?

I freeze.

Wait.

Nothing.

Page 532. There it is.

Aha!

And oh ho, even!

Now, Hammerrocker, Edith.

Page 347.

"Here is our library, all tidy and neat."

Oh great! Mr. Zumwalt!

Remember, Conor, page 347, 347.

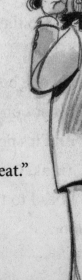

I duck behind the last bookcase. Because I do not want to go to the Special Jail for Boys Who Are Not Supposed to Be in the Library After School.

"Notice how the bookshelves are clear. The books are dust free. I will soon arrange them in size order instead of by alphabet." Mr. Zumwalt turns slowly, taping everything.

Please, oh please, don't film the boy hiding in nonfiction.

"Now we will go to the cafeteria so you can see

it as it should be—free of students."

Yes, leave.

"Oh no, what is this?" Mr. Zumwalt stops.

Oh no.

"A book lying on a table for no reason? How messy." Mr. Zumwalt picks up the book. My book. Puts in under his arm.

Which is better than me in the same place.

Molly McGuire appears at the door.

"The tables are all lined up, washed and ready to go," she says. "If it's okay, I'm leaving."

"Thank you, Miss McGuire. I'll be right there." Mr. Zumwalt lays the book down on the nearest shelf.

"No one else is in the school," she says. "Do you want me to lock the door?"

"That would be very good, thank you," Mr. Zumwalt says.

"I'll get my things then."

He leaves, she heads down the hall.

I've got a minute or two before I am locked in the library.

I see the book way up high. Where I can't read page 347.

Aaarggghhh.

Molly McGuire will be back soon.

She'd help me.

But the Zumwalt could show up at any second.

I break Jack's land-speed record as I run for the door.

"Conor, for the ninety-ninth time, I will call Molly McGuire to see if she can let us into the school. But that will be after this party, for which we are late," my mom says as she drives Jack, Timmy, Bella, and me.

"What is it we're supposed to do?" I ask.

"Mrs. Magoolaghan said Mugsy really wants you three to help Murphy with the games. Isn't that sweet?"

"Mugsy? Sweet?"

"I don't think this is what Mugsy wants," Bella says, fixing the skirt on her green tutu. "But it's my favorite green."

"I don't understand," I tell Bella. This has happened before.

"Mugsy wants everyone to wear green and

black to the party," Bella explains.

Green? Black?

"Mom, where is this party?" I ask.

"Right here, at the Bayou Nature Sanctuary," she answers as she turns down the dirt road. "They have a little party center in a clearing."

"I've got a bad feeling about this," I say.

"I know," Timmy says. "It's probably too hot for ice-cream cake."

"Who are all those kids with painted faces?" Jack asks.

Uh-oh.

Freaky Joe Rule Number Eight: When You Have a Bad Feeling About Something, Pay Attention.

Right now Murphy and I are pulling on the string while the kids, all of whom have faces painted green and black to match their clothing, try to break open the piñata. Which is a bomber plane full of candy.

Actually, Bella's painted green-and-black rainbows and green-and-black daisies on her face. But the rest of them are pretty scary-looking.

Okay, Dwayne's not scary. He looks like a green crayon.

We are all still wet from helping with the water-balloon game. Which consisted of throwing water balloons at the big kids. Water balloons that looked exactly like hand grenades.

Timmy and Jack put candles on the cake. The cake in the shape of a tank.

Mugsy gets off a great swing, breaking the piñata open.

"Incoming," she yells.

"One more game before we have the cake," Mrs. Magoolaghan announces.

"All right!" Mugsy begins to jump up and down. "Time for the hunt."

"Are you having a treasure hunt, sweetie?" my mom asks.

"No, we're hunting for escaped enemy prisoners," Mugsy answers. "But we'll give you a head start," she says.

Huh?

"You don't have to do this, honey," my mom yells as Jack, Timmy, Murphy, and I hightail it down the road. Soon to be followed by a screaming horde of small scary people. And one ballerina.

"They cannot catch the Smart Guys," Jack swears.

"There they are!" Mugsy screams.

"Get them!" the others yell with candy-covered mouths.

"I'm not getting my brother," Bella yells.

"Time for a land-speed record!" I tell everyone. "Split up and meet back at the party."

This seems like a simple idea, till I lose the path a short ways back. At least the yells

of the Wild Children seem to be going away from me.

Though I thought I heard Jack screaming, "Nooooooo!"

That can't be good.

And I can't be lost. But I might be.

I'll follow the bayou, which will lead me back.

The water is down low today. Way low. I don't know if I could hit it with a rock from here. It's hard to believe it was up here, over the banks and out on the road this spring.

A heron stands in the stream, eating something that I'm sure only herons like. Or Timmy.

There's a clearing up ahead. But it's the wrong one. This one has a bench looking out over the bayou. And a big rock with a bronze marker with words and a picture of someone. Holding something.

A person who looks familiar.

I lean in to read. And I cannot believe my eyes.

Bingo.

Chapter Fourteen

When It Rains, It Pours

"Molly can talk to you," my mom says as she hands me the phone. "Do you want to go to the school?"

"I don't know yet," I answer.

"Well, I owe you," my mom says.

"I think you owe Jack more."

"It did take a while to get him out of that tree," my mom admits. "Mugsy certainly knows a lot of different knots."

I ask Molly McGuire my first question. Her answer is *yes*.

Bingo.

I ask her my second question. Her answer is *no*.

Interesting.

• • • •

It'll be good to check *A History of Prater County from Then Till Now* tomorrow at school. But everything that Molly McGuire knows is enough to get me started.

But I have a lot of writing to do. And fast. Because we'll have to rehearse today.

And I still have to decide what to do about what I read on page 532.

And just how would that explain the hamsters in the gym? And the books?

In his glass case in The Secret Place, Bob is going nuts.

Of course he would, I think. Now that I know what I know.

"Someone's coming," I tell Bella.

Clang!

"Jack's here," she says. "So Timmy will be next."

"What's the matter?" Jack asks. "You said it's an emergency."

"I bought extra supplies," Timmy says as he dumps two big brown bags on the floor.

"We're here," Murphy announces.

"No!" Jack yells as he sees Mugsy.

"Tell Jack you won't hurt him," Murphy tells Mugsy.

"We are going to be savers of the day," Bella announces.

My mom comes in with the papers. "Here you go, a copy for everyone."

"Okay team, we have a lot of work and only two days to do it in. And one of them's a school day." I hand out the papers.

"You said an emergency, Conor, not work," Jack complains.

"Since everyone has more than one part, I think we should do it again," I announce on Monday after dinner. "Tomorrow is the assembly."

"Noooo!" everyone answers.

"Conor, this is good enough," my mom insists as she finishes sewing the hem on the dress Murphy is wearing.

"But the Sharks . . . ," I begin.

"Are going down tomorrow," my mom insists. "And your hamster is falling asleep."

"Bob's running around," Jack says.

"The other one, Jack." Timmy points.

"Oh."

Tuesday morning. Timmy, Jack, and I carry all our big stuff to the cafeteria.

"We'll put them back here on the stage." I push them up against the wall.

"But are we ready?" Timmy asks.

"Absolutely," I say.

Freaky Joe Rule Number Sixteen: Be Confident. It Can't Hurt.

But I still don't know what Freaky Joe would say about page 532.

And I've been too busy to try to find out.

Jake and Mick stand beside Jeremiah as he finishes his presentation. Around their necks are homemade shark's heads with big shark's teeth. Which I think are supposed to look scary, but instead make it look like their heads are sitting inside a broken eggshell.

"And that is why we think a shark is the perfect symbol of our school. So vote for deadly. Vote for scary. Vote for a lot of teeth. Vote Sharks."

Lots of loud clapping. Not good.

Jeremiah hands the microphone to Mr. Zumwalt.

"And now we will hear from Conor Moloney as to why we should keep *Hamsters* as our school name," he says. "Hamsters," he adds as he puts the mike in the stand, saying the word as if it was the stupidest thing on the planet Earth.

"Who is that guy?" Mugsy's words carry out behind the stage curtain.

I begin.

"I am not here to ask you to vote for Hamsters. I am here to ask you to please keep the Hammerrocker Hamster as a symbol of our school. For we should be proud to bear the name of one of Houston's bravest heroes."

Jack and Timmy open the curtain on cue. Molly McGuire comes to the corner of the stage. She sings.

"Oh, first the sky was clear
On that awful day.
What was to come, oh none could say."

"Yes," I say, "it was an ordinary day in our city. A day in our city's past, a day when our great-grandmothers would have been little girls. A day of work and play before the afternoon rains started."

With big bows on their heads, Mugsy and Bella and Jack skip around the stage. Timmy rakes and hoes.

They leave as Molly sings again.

> "All could have been lost,
> Yes, everyone's home,
> By the terrible rains
> From the heavenly dome."

Jack and Timmy bring out a desk. And a chair. And Bob in his hamster world.

Murphy, wearing a grown-up dress and glasses, sits down and pretends to read. I go on with the story.

"It rained harder than it had ever rained before. And then rained some more. While the people slept, the bayous filled up. In her little home, Edith R. Hammerrocker, a young librarian, was working late. She heard the heavy rain as she fell asleep reading."

Murphy's head hits the table with a thump.

"But for one person,
Whose brave tale I will now tell,
Who with her buddy did sound
The warning bell,"

Molly McGuire sings.

"Close one of the curtains, Jack." Timmy whispers loud enough to be heard in the back.

Murphy's half of the stage disappears.

"But one creature was not asleep all night. One very smart creature who could tell something was wrong."

Jack and Timmy push our big box onto the
other half of the stage. We had cut out the sides
of the box and covered them with plastic to
make it look like a giant hamster cage. With
Bella the hamster inside.

"This creature was Edith Hammerrocker's pet hamster, Babette. Animals know when things are wrong in the natural world. When a hurricane comes, seagulls land on islands, turning to face the wind. Otters warn us of tidal waves. Beetles' behavior predicts earthquakes. And Babette knew the water was rising in the bayou that night. And that her beloved Edith was in danger."

In her hamster cage, Bella begins to run around. Jump up and down. Turn hamster cartwheels. Throw hamster paper up into the air. Make loud hamster noises.

"And still the water rose higher."

The water, which is Jack, Timmy, and Mugsy under a big blue sheet, crawls across the stage.

"Babette was desperate. She yelled little hamster yells. She banged her head on the glass and scratched the walls of her cage. And Edith woke up."

The first-graders begin to cheer.

"What is it, what's wrong, Babette?" Murphy's voice asks.

Bella jumps up and down, pointing at the floor. The water comes back out, rolling a little as it goes across the stage and disappears.

"Water in the cottage? What can be wrong?" Murphy asks.

"Timmy, the paper says close the curtain now," Jack yells.

"Oh Edith, oh Edith,
You and Babette did save us all,
When you rang the church bell
To give the warning call,"

Molly sings as the curtain closes.

"Edith looked out into the stormy night," I go on. "She saw the water from a flooded bayou coming down the street. Bravely she set out into the night, with Babette safely in her pocket. The wind and rain pushed them back. But Edith pushed on."

"Now we should open it," Jack yells again.

The cage is gone from the stage. Murphy pushes her way across, bent in half. The water wraps around her legs. The water gets a little tangled up in itself. Murphy goes down. The water says, "Ow."

"She fell time and again," I quickly add. "But she and brave Babette made it to the church, climbed up to the tower, and rang the bell over and over, waking the citizens of the town. They ran from their homes to see the flood coming."

Jack, Timmy, Bella, and Mugsy run onstage in old-fashioned nightshirts with old-fashioned sleeping caps on their heads.

"Everyone and their cows quickly ran for higher ground. No one was lost because of Edith and Babette. The town never forgot what they did. They put a bench and a plaque out by where the bayou flooded. And when Edith retired after many, many years as a librarian, they decided to name a school for her. And in honor of Babette, they named the school mascot the Hammerrocker Hamster."

More cheering starts.

"For the school, they had a portrait painted of Edith and Babette. With a special frame made of wood that was washed up in the flood." I don't take the time to explain that the special frame was too big, and hid Babette. Molly says she's going to fix it anyway.

"We should not change our name," I finish. "We should be proud of our school name, and proud of our mascot: the brave, brave Babette."

The actors join Molly at the microphone. They begin to chant:

"Babette, Babette, she's the one, saved the day for everyone!"

"Vote Hamster. Vote for Babette!" I shout.

The students join in:

"Babette, Babette, she's the one, saved the day for everyone."

Someone calls out "Hamsters rock!" Mom.

The whole cafeteria sings, "Hamsters rock! Hamsters rock!"

Mr. Zumwalt does not look happy. He does his bent leg, elbows out run to the front.

"That will be enough," he tells me. "I'll have that microphone. We still have to vote."

"Hammerrocker Hamster Hello!" Molly McGuire calls out.

The students leap to their feet, hold their arms out in front, wiggle all ten fingers, bare their teeth, and shake their heads.

"Hamsters! Hmmmm! Hamsters! Hmmmm!" they yell.

Just as Mr. Zumwalt turns to face them.

"Babette! Babette!"

"Hamsters! Hamsters!"

He freezes. "Noooo!" he yells. "No Hamsters!" Mr. Zumwalt hollers. He begins to talk into the mike. "I've tried to stop you. I've put out signs to show everyone the truth: Hamsters are terrible! The letter H was meant to warn you. Hamsters are terrifying. No little children should be called *Hamsters*! Or be anywhere around hamsters!" He begins to wave his arms around. Like he's pushing something away. As if that something is all over him. On his face, on his arms.

Poor, poor Zoot Zumwalt.

Everyone stands quiet for a moment.

"Hamsters still rock!" someone yells.

The kids yell it out. Wave their hands in the Hamster Hello.

"No more!" Mr. Zumwalt yells as he runs from the cafeteria. "No more hamsters!"

Everyone stares for a few moments.

"Hey look," Jack points out the window.

"That guy is running away down the street," Mugsy says.

"Where's Mr. Zumwalt going?" Timmy asks.

Poor Zoot, I think again.

"Let's sing Babette's song one more time," Molly says.

The whole school answers her when she sings, "Oh, first the sky was clear on that awful day."

I wonder what the sky was like on Mr. Zumwalt's awful day.

Mr. Lefty comes to the front of the cafeteria. "Since Mr. Zumwalt has gone, I'll pinch hit. We will now vote for the school mascot."

Mr. Lefty says four times, "All in favor of . . ."

The other names get a few votes. But Edith and Babette win the day.

"Yes!" I pump my arm up and down.

"End zone dance!" Timmy yells. Bella and Mugsy join in on stage.

"Nightshirt hula," Jack calls. Molly McGuire does that one.

The students do one or the other.

I have to say things are looking good here at the Edith R. Hammerrocker Elementary School. Home of the Hamsters.

Chapter Fifteen

This Is Where the End Goes

"This was one of the best school days ever," Timmy says as he lies on the floor of The Secret Place a week later.

"An ice-cream party is pretty cool in school," Jack agrees.

"Those were nice people to give us a prize," Timmy says as he rubs his stomach.

Some people from the company that makes Doesn't That Smell Clean? were at our school today. They told us all in assembly that they had come to give us a special prize.

It seems that in his rush to send in his video for the contest, Mr. Zumwalt made a mistake. And sent in the wrong one. The one with the hamsters in the gym, and the books on the floor of the library, and the library ceiling, not to mention Mugsy, Mikey, and Dwayne in the library case.

"We laughed so hard," the Doesn't That Smell Clean? man said, "that we had to award you a special prize, an ice-cream party, for being the funniest school."

He did seem a little disappointed not to meet Mr. Zumwalt.

Mr. Lefty explained that Mr. Zumwalt had decided to take a break from working in schools. He was now working for the Anti-Rodent Society.

"We are waiting to hear who will be our new principal," Mr. Lefty explained. "Until then Mrs. Stern is acting principal."

"I can't believe Mr. Zumwalt was really in a book," Jack says.

"Page five hundred thirty-two," I tell him. "I was looking for Edith Hammerrocker when I saw his name in the index. So I decided to check it out."

"It would be cool to be in a book," Timmy says.

"Not because you had something awful happen to you in a barn full of hamsters when you were a kid," I suggest.

"I would not have been scared," Jack insists.

"Anyone would have been scared."

"Exactly what happened?" Timmy asks.

I tell them what I read. "There was a abandoned barn on that old farm out by the bayou. There was a 'No Trespassing' sign, but Zoot and his friends went there anyway. And someone double dared Zoot to go into the barn. Foolishly, he agreed. So he climbed in the upper window. It was too dark to see all the way to the bottom. Zoot tried to climb down. But he lost his balance, slipping and sliding down to the floor."

"This is not good," Jack admits.

"Really not good," I explain. "Because when

the farm was abandoned, and all the animals taken, two creatures were left behind. The farmer's son had two pet hamsters who had crawled up into the walls. No one knew they were there. But they were. And as time went on there were more hamsters. And more. By the time Zoot Zumwalt slid to the floor of the barn, there were hundreds and hundreds. Maybe thousands of hamsters. Who all ran over to see what had come down from the high window. Hamsters everywhere, and a lot of them on top of Zoot."

"I wonder what they ate to stay alive," Timmy wonders.

"The book called it The Horrible Hamster Incident. When Zoot finally got to his feet and ran out the door, he left it open. And out the hamsters ran. They were everywhere. It took weeks and weeks to collect them. And they probably never got them all. And Mr. Zumwalt

was away at a special hospital for weeks and weeks."

"So Mr. Zumwalt made those hamsters in the gym, and the letter H in the library, to get the other kids mad at us. So they would not vote for

Hamsters," Jack says. "He might have changed his mind if he had only met Bob." Jack sticks his nose up close. Bob tries to bite it through the glass.

"Why did Molly McGuire write the words on the board?" Timmy asks.

"Because she was hoping it would make someone find out about Edith, and stop Mr. Zumwalt. She knew about Edith from that old folk song," I answer.

"Why didn't she just stop him?" Jack asks.

"Because she thought the kids should save their own school. At least that's what she told me."

"That seems fair," Timmy admits.

"And I think you can say we did do it," says Jack.

"Conor was the one who really saved the day," Timmy points out.

"The Freaky Joe Club saved the day," I insist. "Which is what we're supposed to do."

"So now do we get to see inside the book?" Timmy points at the Red Book, the real and true Secret Files.

"The Smart Guys are good to go," Jack says.

I think they are ready. Maybe not for all of it. But for some.

I open the lock, unwrap the chain, and start at the back. "Here is where I've entered our cases," I show them.

I turn the pages back a little. "And here is the person who told me about Freaky Joe."

"Aha!" says Jack.

"I knew it," Timmy shouts.

"So did I," Jack says.

"No, you didn't, Copycat Boy," Timmy insists.

"Did too, Candy Boy," Jack tells him. As he jumps on his head.

And Timmy rolls on the floor.

And Riley jumps on his back.

I wait. They'll be done soon.

A little while later I finish Sir Chester and Chuck, and put them on the shelf. I pick up the new Remington Reedmarsh I've been waiting to read. One book finished. One mystery solved. One school saved. And a new book in front of me. A new mystery waiting for me. Things are definitely looking good.

Want things to start going your way?
Don't forget to read the next adventure of

The Freaky Joe Club

Secret File #5:

The Mystery of the Disappearing Dinosaurs